This book belongs to:

....

Teeheehee

For Tim, Nicholas, Annabelle and Katherine
JR

For Duncan, Michael, Mumsie and Dad
CB

Can you spot
where I'm hiding
on every page?

Published by Two Pups
an imprint of Burnet Media

Burnet Media is the publisher
of Mercury, Two Dogs and
Two Pups books
info@burnetmedia.co.za
www.burnetmedia.co.za
PO Box 53557, Kenilworth, 7745,
South Africa

First published 2016
1 3 5 7 9 8 6 4 2

Text © 2016 Julia Richman
Illustrations © 2016
Celeste Beckerling

Distributed by Jacana Media
www.jacana.co.za

Printed and bound by
Tandym Print
www.tandym.co.za

ISBN 9781928230434

Burnet Media | TWO PUPS

A Huddle of Hippos

and other cool collective nouns for animals

Hi, I'm Sam. Are you ready for an exciting safari adventure? Then come with me!

Julia Richman

Illustrated by Celeste Beckerling

Hooray!

My first sighting of the day.
And it's a big surprise, I have to say.
It's the happiest of hippos in a group hug,
Mum can't believe her eyes
and dad's spotted
a lady bug.

And what do we have here?
These dudes are in stitches.
A **cackle of hyenas**?
I'd say more like cackling witches.

What's so funny?
Pray do tell?
What's got you lot under
such a laughing spell?

Peekaboo!

What about the
troop of monkeys
hiding in this tree?
How many of these little guys
do you think you can see?

Here's a **herd of elephants** rolling in the mud.
The pretty one is chatting to the big giraffe stud.

The poor **flight of doves** got such a big fright.

The boogying
leap of leopards,
an absolute hit.

Mighty fine dancers,
you have to admit...

And Dad's even doing his little bit!

A **dazzle of zebras** and a **shimmer of butterflies**...

What an exciting safari, I'm having such fun!

Click!

A **stand of flamingoes**, all pretty in pink.

Some of them skiing, don't miss it, don't blink!

And who else is hiding out at the watering hole today?

Eeeeek!
A not-so-friendly
float of crocodiles
coming out to play.

A **prickle of porcupines**,
what a lucky sight.
Mum says they only ever
come out at night.

Look how their quills
prick that big
cloud of bats.
Now the bats will go mad...
Hold on to your hats!

Here's a
pride of lions,
noses in the air.

One's eating steak tartare
and sitting on a chair.

And
who's that
I see over there?

A **muster of peacocks** and a **mischief of mice**...

The rodents
look naughty
and the
peacocks have lice!

And this
pack of wild dogs
you have to admire.

Wearing ballet leotards,
sitting by the fire.

'All right, young man,
    time to go home,' says Dad.
'We'll come again soon,
    so don't be too sad.'

But I'm still searching for
        what more I can spy...

A **bed of snakes**, look!
    And a **scurry of squirrels**,
                bye-bye!

And then we're off, racing
        through the spooky dark night...

Animal shadows
        and eyes shining
in the African moonlight.

Activity page

A swarm of ....

A cackle of ....

A .... of flamingoes

A cloud of ....

A .... of lions

A .... of crocodiles

A .... of snakes

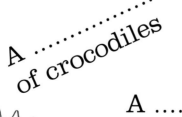